HELMUT RAZOR
Serial Killer

by

Robbie Moffat

PALM TREE PUBLISHING

PALM TREE PUBLISHING
Paisley, Scotland Pa1 1TJ

© Robbie Moffat 2019

First published in paperback JANUARY 2019

Typeset: Verdana 12pt

ISBN-10: 0 907282 58 X
ISBN-13: 9780907282587

PREFACE

This story is no romance. Its brutal, gruesome, horrible and totally indefensible. However, it is action, misadventure and things gone wrong, and as such, it is a story about mayhem and murder.

For this kind of story there is always an audience obsessed with crime, blood and misogyny. If there is a moral, then it must be that the reader following the actions of our anti-hero will not be compelled to commit the same acts and be ever watchful for those who do.

DEDICATION

For my good friend, Gabriella.

1

"What's wrong with me?"
A tired male voice trails off, waits for a response.
"You had a bad childhood, Muti ..."
The older female voice is discoloured by guilt and regret.
The sound of passing cars drowns out her long sigh as she lights a cigarette and puts it to her over painted lips.
"The other kids didn't like you. I don't know why. You were a lovely little boy."
Helmut Razor's eyes narrow as he glances sideways to his mother.
"I was never a nice boy!"
"I blame your father. He was a brute of a man with his English ways and rough hands. When I met him I thought he was the most handsome man I had ever met. Then again I was just a young girl, easily impressed by foreigners."
Helmut's hands tighten on the steering wheel.
His knuckles are tattooed. On his right hand are the letters H...E...L...L and his left hand R...A...Z...R.
He says nothing ... but his eyes are

dark and glaring.

He is back to being six years old, his father brutally beating him senseless. His mother is hunched upstairs on the landing sucking on a half-spent cigarette. Helmut is dragged across the kitchen floor and thrust into a cupboard under the sink.

"I hated living in Bradford." Gisela Razor lets out a long stream of fag smoke that curls around her sixty year old mouth and clings to the roof of the Volkswagen Beetle they are travelling in.

"You're not going back there, mother. If I went back to Bradford I wouldn't be responsible for what I did …."

"Children can be cruel, Helmut. You must learn to forgive. Just for once, try to stay out of trouble. You're twenty two years old. You need to grow up. I'm tired of moving on."

"I didn't like Munich … the smell of beer everywhere." It was true. Every turn of the street and the stench of a brewery close-by would make him want to vomit.

Gisela's face brightens, she feels optimistic "They say Brighton is a nice town."

Ahead through the windscreen is the sea. Their old beat-up German built car rolls onwards towards the blue beyond. It is laden with their few possessions – everything they own – stuffed into front luggage compartment, the back-seat or strapped to the roof.

They are just another pair of economic migrants looking for a better life than the one they are running from.

*

The room they have rented is shabby and dilapidated. There is mould in the corners of the damp walls and peeling wallpaper. Gisela stands at the bay window smoking a cigarette. She is watching her son unload the car.

Down in the street, Helmut has a concealed Samurai sword in his hand wrapped in a blanket. He looks up and sees his mother watching him. "Why can't she ever relax" he mutters to himself.

He tucks the sword under his arm and glances down the street – a row of peeling white-washed Victorian houses turned into people-businesses with their To Let and B&B signs jutting out, competing with one another to lure the poor and destitute with their cheap advertising.

The landlady Mrs. Hackett is standing on the boarding house steps. She smiles at him as he mounts the steps. "You're a good looking foreigner." He smiles back, passes silently. She looks up, catches Gisela looking down at her.

Back up in the flat, Helmut enters the room and deposits on the floor the last load, a box of his mother's shoes.

"Two hundred and forty pounds a week, Muti." she bemoans. "How are we going to pay for that week on week?"

"I'll find a way. I always do." His answer is shifty and Gisela knows it.

"I don't like your ways, Muti. I want to be respectable."

"How are we going to be respectable living in a street like this?"

"We will make it a home, son. A little bit of paint here and there. We'll keep to ourselves … live a quite life."

"Yes, mama." He doesn't seem to believe her. He turns over a brown-stained queen sized divan bed mattress. The other side is the same. "This is disgusting."

"I want no nonsense, Helmut. You promised me. You have to stay away from young people. They are bad and they always get you into trouble."

"Yes, mama." He has heard it all before.

"And no beer drinking …. You promise me?"

Helmut nods as if he has heard it a hundred times.

"Where do you want to sleep, mama?"

"By the window. It reminds me of my childhood. I grew up looking at the Alps from my bed."

Helmut wheels the bed over to the window. He straightens. Gisela tests the bed with her hand. "This is not fit for someone my age," she whimpers.

"I'll speak to the landlady about replacing it, mama."

"Danke". She kisses him on the lips. "Where will you sleep, darling?"

"I'll sleep over there." He points to small alcove near the kitchen where there is a fold-up bed.

Gisela takes the last cigarette from a crumpled packet. "Do we have enough money for fish and chips tonight." She inspects the small cooker in the kitchenette looking for a light. "I don't feel like cooking."

"Do you want some wine too, mama?" Helmut knows his mother inside out.

"Just a cheap bottle. White. Riesling. They have that everywhere nowadays."

"I know what you like." he puts on his leather jacket which has a tear on the left sleeve.

"And some cigarettes, son."

"Yes, mama."

Helmut is walking the streets, taking in his new surroundings. It is not all decay and as depressed as he first thought. Here and there are bright lights and affluent refuges from the grim and down at heel facades of most of the shops.

He picks up a bottle of Riesling and a couple of cans of beer from an off-license. Outside the shop he cracks open one of the cans and guzzles it. He smacks his lips in satisfaction, drains the rest of the can, and throws it over a hedge. He opens his second can. He downs it just as fast, stopping only once for breath. He throws the second can over the hedge.

Two teenage girls, one blonde, one brunette, totter towards him in six-inch high heels and short skirts. They are barely adults. The blonde whispers something to her mate. The brunette slips her a tenner. The blonde takes from her pocket another tenner, and followed by the brunette approaches Helmut.

"Heh, mister. If I give you twenty can you get us some cider?"

"What's in it for me?"

They giggle.

"No, I mean it." He is serious.

"Are you a perv or something?" the brunette jokes.

"No, of course not. Just think you are two stunning looking birds."

"You don't half speak like my dad," the blonde cackles.

"Tell you what." Helmut is growing in confidence "If I get you the cider, how about you show me the pier?"

"What are you on?" the blonde laughs.

"I'm new in town. What's your names?"

"Alice." The blonde.

"Brenda." The brunette

"Alright Alice and Brenda. You look as though you'd be up for an adventure. Am I right or what?"

"Maybe." Alice looks him in the eyes. She is flirting with him. "What you sez, Brenda?"

"Don't know ..."

Helmut holds up his car key. "I've got a car. You can get pissed in my back seat."

Brenda's resistance evaporates. "Yeah, alright." Alice hands Helmut the two ten-pound notes.

"Sure you don't want something stronger than cider?"

"No way. We get pissed no probs on cider. Get the really strong stuff will ya?"

Brenda produces another tenner. "And get us twenty fags."

Helmut smiles. "For a tenner, you'll be lucky. Maybe I'll make up the difference." He takes the money.

*

Helmut is driving.

Alice is in the front swigging from a large cider bottle. Brenda steals it from her.

"Heh, Brenda!" Alice snatches it back.

"Now, now, girls. There's loads of bottles. Open another one. Get one for me too!"

Brenda hands Helmut a bottle. He glugs at it. "Cmon, you slags! Drink up!"

They compete to see who finishes their drink first. Helmut wins.

"You bastard! You're trying to get us drunk!"

"Correct. And you're a bolshie little mouthful!"

"Of course I am. And you like it! Isn't that right?"

They look at each other, burst into a fit of laughter.

"How old are you?"

"I'm seventeen. Brenda's sixteen."

"I'm seventeen next week." Brenda corrects her.

"Are you virgins?"

"No way! Neither of us. Brenda's the school bike."

"You proud of that, Brenda?"

"Yeah, I am. All those little pricks!"

They laugh.

"What's your name?" Alice is now high on the cider.

"I'm Bob. Bob the Builder!"

They all burst out laughing.

"Naw, seriously, Bob. Tell us your name!"

"It's Bob. Bob Butcher."

"You're making that up!" Brenda is drunk.

"No. It's true. Want to see my knife?"

They girls go into giggles again.

"Where's this pier then?"

"Stuff that. You want a shag don't you?" Alice gives him a lingering look.

"You offering?"

"Maybe." Alice puts her hand on Helmut's thigh. "Why don't you turn left here and we can go up the woods?"

"You alright with that, Brenda?" Helmut asks.

Brenda is finishing off a second bottle of cider. She is really pissed.

"Don't mind."

The car is parked up in a clump of trees. It is very dark. The interior car light is on but the front passenger door is open. Helmut's bare legs are out of the car. Alice is riding on his lap with her back to him.

"What's taking you so long?" Alice is getting sore. "Its starting to hurt."

"Keep going ….." Helmut is riding his luck.

Brenda is passed out in the back seat.

Alice is beginning to feel very uncomfortable. "I'm worried about Brenda."

"She's sleeping it off."

Alice is concerned. "It's not like her." Alice stops her riding movements.

"Why've you stopped? C'mon, I haven't given you a baby yet!" He holds her by the throat, gets her to move up and down again, go with his movement.

"Have you put something in Brenda's drink?" Alice is struggling to breathe.

"Why would I do that, you little tart?"

Alice reacts to his tone. She stops dead. She tries to remove his hand from her throat, push it on to her breast. Helmut does not resist and realises that the fun is over. His free hand reaches under the car seat.

Alice is sobering up. She starts to prise herself off Helmut.

There is a glint of steel.

Helmut puts a knife to Alice's throat. It is a long sharp butcher's knife.

Alice freezes in terror.

"I'm not finished yet. Move." He thrusts his hips.

Alice is terrified.

"I said move!" He thrusts again.

Alice moves abruptly. He restrains her.

"Nice and slow. Just nice and slow. You young ones need to learn how to slow down."

The knife is now restricting her breathing. A small drop of blood appears on the blade of the knife. Alice's eyes are sunken. She quickens in fear.

"Nice and slow ….."

"Don't kill me … Please don't kill me. Please."

"I like you, Alice. I don't kill people I like unless they don't like me. Do you like me, Alice?"

"Yes, I like you."

"Really like me?"

"Yes."

"Do you love me?"

"What do you mean …." She is trying to understand the question but is so confused she no longer knows what she is saying.

"Do you love me?"

"Yes …."

"Then let me hear you say it."

"Say what …. I don't understand." She is crying for her life.

"Say to me … I love you, Bob."

Alice, in full tears, is still on Helmut's lap, moving. Helmut is climaxing. His legs are tensing. A spot of blood falls on to one of Alice's thighs.

Then another.

And another.

Helmut groans.

The knife slices across Alice's throat. He throws her off. She falls head first out of the car. She disappears into the dark.

Brenda stirs in the back. Helmut gets out of the car. He pulls back the front seat, grabs Brenda by the front of her blouse, jerks her out into the woods. He throws her on top of Alice who is lying on the ground gurgling. She starts to whimper as she realises what is happening.

Helmut is astride her.

"This is your last bike ride, you dozy little cow. Welcome to the abattoir." He brings the knife down on her. He repeatedly stabs her again and again. He slashes and slashes. He is awash with blood as he continues to slash.

*

Gisela is half asleep on her bed as Helmut enters the room. He is carrying a parcel of fish and chips and the bottle of Riesling. Gisela stirs, turns towards him.

"What time is it, Muti?"

"Late, mama."

"Where have you been?"

"I got lost. Brighton's a big town."

Gisela sits up in the bed.

"I've got fish and chips."

"I can smell it." She straightens her clothes. Helmut divides the fish and chips onto two plates. He opens the bottle, pours his mother some wine into a plastic cup.

"I need a smoke." It is a demand rather than a statement of desire.

"I have them here." He hands his mother a fresh pack of twenty.

"Your favourite brand of English cigarettes."

"You are a good boy." She kisses him on the cheek.

"Maybe we could visit the pier tomorrow, mama?"

"You should be looking for work?" Her hands are shaking and she struggles to tear open the packet of cigarettes.

"We'll be fine. Its a Saturday. We can afford to take one day off in life." He starts into his fish and chips.

Gisela strikes a match, tries to light a cigarette.

"I need to get you a lighter," Helmut observes. He takes the match box from her hand, strikes a match for her.

"What would I do without you, Muti?"

"I don't know, mama." Gisela takes a long draw on the cigarette. "Eat your fish and chips, mama."

Gisela takes another long draw on her cigarette, exhales. She slowly looks down at fish supper. She makes a face. "I'm not hungry now. Wrap it up. I'll have it tomorrow."

Helmut reluctantly does as he is

told. She takes a long sip of her wine, looks out of the window.

"There's a good view from this window."

"You said that before."

"Its the lights. So many lights. What are those people doing burning all that electricity? Its a waste. In Germany we would switch off half of them."

Helmut pulls the curtains.

"Helmut! I didn't say I didn't like the light show."

"I'm getting cold, mama." He just wants to shut out the night's events.

"Cold? Its in your mind! Open the curtains!"

Helmut reluctantly reopens the curtains. He wraps his arms around himself."I'm tired, I'm going to bed."

"You can be such a spoilt little boy."

"Stop it, mama. You have your cigarettes and wine. I'm going to bed." He crosses the room towards his bed.

"Where's my kiss?" she demands.

Helmut stops, turns slowly back towards his mother. Gisela taps her cheek. "You know that I love you. Don't be cross with mama." Helmut bends and kisses her on the cheek.

"Guten nacht, mutter."

"Guten nacht, liebschen."

Helmut crosses the room to his fold down bed. Sits on it, starts to undress. Gisela slowly pulls her cigarette away from her mouth, stubs it out.

"Perhaps I'll sleep tonight."

"I hope so, mama."

"I'm glad we got out of Germany. Its a new beginning. All our troubles are behind us. Yes, lets go to the pier tomorrow. We can have tea!"

Helmut settles in his bed. He stares up at the ceiling at the bare eco-light bulb. Gisela is humming. Helmut turns away to shut her humming out. She is humming *Lille Marlene*. He puts his hands over his ears.

2

The sound of lapping water. There is a strong breeze. Gisela is on her son's arm as they stroll up the pier. She is wearing an elegant wide brimmed hat that could once have been worn at the Royal Enclosure at Ascot, though not by Gisela. In contrast, Helmut looks very ordinary and nondescript.

A gust of wind catches Gisela's hat, whips it from her head. The hat blows across the boardwalk to lodge against the pier rail.

"Helmut!"

"I'll get it, mama."

He runs towards the hat. As he reaches for it, it goes over the edge. Helmut looks over the rail. The hat floats down – lands on the sand below. Gisela joins her son.

"I'll get it, mama. You stay here."

Helmut starts back down the pier towards the entrance. Gisela looks over the rail again. A barefooted young couple are nearby. The girl sees the hat and points. The hat is blowing along the sand. The boy breaks into a run, chases the hat, crushes it into the sand with his foot.

Gisela utters a little cry of despair at the treatment of her beautiful hat. The boy places the hat on the girl's head. She has to hold it on with her hand as the breeze is strong. The couple kiss.

From above Gisela is waving down at them. They break from their embrace, see her. The boy gives her two fingers.

Gisela drops her arm, waits to see if they will return the hat to her. Instead, the young couple kick sand at one another, chase one another under the pier. Gisela loses sight of them.

Under the pier, the couple are kissing. The girl is holding the hat in her hand and is hitting him with it as he tickles her. Helmut appears, sees them. He halts, thinks for a moment. He is not sure what to do.

He looks about. The rest of the beach is deserted except for a man with a dog going away from the pier.

He looks at his hands, flexes them.

The young couple see him, straighten themselves. The boy takes the girl's hand and starts to lead her back the way they have come.

"Excuse me!" Helmut's shout is barely hard over the sound of the lapping waves and the breeze. "Oiiii you!" The boy turns and takes up a provocative stance.

"You talking to me, mate!"

Helmut catches up with the couple.
"Yeah, I am. You've got my mother's hat."

The boy takes the hat from the girl, looks in the headband for a name. "No name on it, mate. Finders keepers." The boy stares Helmut out. The girl gets behind him.

"What's your name then, sonny?"

"You gonna report me to the rossers for picking up litter." He laughs at his own joke.

"I asked you your name?"

"It's Robin. What's yours then? Batman?"

"Try to be nice, Colin." The girl is uneasy.

"Shut it, Doreen. This geezer is messin' with the wrong fella."

"I'm asking you nicely, Colin." Helmut extends his hand for the hat. "She doesn't want the hat."

Colin turns and puts it on Doreen's head. "It belongs to her now. See, don't she look a peach?"

"She's an ugly cow."

"What'd you say? Say that again and I'm gonna kill ya!" Colin produces a switch-blade from his pocket, flicks it open.

"Colin!" Doreen snatches the hat off

her head and thrusts it at Helmut.
"He's on crack, mister. He don't
mean no harm, honest."

"That's alight then. I'll let him off."
Helmut takes the hat, looks at it,
turns to go. He stops, notices a
small hole in the hat. "Just one
thing. You got to pay for this
damage." He pokes his finger
through the hole.

Colin looks at Helmut wriggling his
finger. Doreen gets between them.
"We don't mean no harm. We're just
young, looking for laughs. You know
how it is?"

"No I don't."

"Get out the way, Dors!" Colin
pushes Doreen aside and lunges at
Helmut's belly with his flick-knife.
Helmut side-steps Colin's lunge, hits
him with his forearm across the
back of his head. Colin goes down.
The knife drops from his hand as he
falls. Helmut picks up the knife. In a
swift movement, he cuts Doreen
across the throat, then lunges the
knife into the back of Colin's neck. It
is all done in a matter of seconds.

Doreen falls to her knees holding
her throat. Colin is already dead.
Helmut rifles Colin's pockets, finds a

flip lighter. He pockets the lighter. He drags Colin's body to the waterline, wades into the water. Colin's body is set adrift.

Helmut returns to Doreen. She is still on her knees in the process of dying. He pushes her over on to her back, She hits the sand and lets out a final gasp. Helmut undoes her belt and removes her jeans and panties. He throws the panties away. He rifles the jean pockets and stuffs some money into his own pocket. He ties the jeans around her legs and drags her towards the water.

He sets her adrift in the tide. He throws the knife far into the sea. He looks up. He can see dark shadows of people walking across the boardwalk. Yet, there is no-one on the beach, not a soul.

Gisela is sitting on a bench smoking. She is agitated, looking about for signs of Helmut. "Here it is, mama." She turns abruptly. Helmut is wet to the waist and holding the hat. "It's almost as good as new." He pokes his finger through the hole.

"That hole is as old as you are. I was careless with one of these the first time I wore it." She holds up her half smoked cigarette, laughs.

She suddenly notices he is wet. "Helmut! We must get you changed!"

"No, mama, I'm fine. Don't make a fuss." He sits down to hide his wet trousers. He crosses his arms to stay warm.

Gisela puts the hat back on her head, ties her scarf around it. "Shall we have afternoon tea? Its the one thing that the English can do right." She stands up and offers up her arm. Helmut rises, loops his arm into his mother's.

"A mother and son on Brighton Pier. We could be in a film." She is free of her worries and concerns. It is a rare moment for her as they stroll down the boardwalk and back towards the town.

*

Gisela is sitting in a tea shop. Helmut enters carrying a shopping bag. He has on a new pair of jeans.

"Is your wet pair in the bag?"

"I threw them away. Ruined by the seawater. This is another pair. See." He opens the bag and shows her a second pair of jeans. "Two for twenty pounds."

"They'll do you for work."

"There's a lot of unemployment here, mama. People come down here form London to sleep on the streets."

"You'll find something. You're good with your hands."

"I don't have any qualifications, mama."

"You're an all rounder, Muti. I know you're schooling was interrupted, but you can do a bit of plumbing, carpentry that kind of work. You can start by asking that woman we are renting from."

Helmut's eyes are downcast. "I don't like this town. Too many kids. You know I don't like kids."

"Now, Helmut. You promised you would behave yourself. You promised me."

"Yes, mama."

"That's a good boy ....."

Gisela is looking about the teashop. There are a number of elderly women done up to the nines with their jewellery and perfect hairstyles. Gisela feels her own hair, is unhappy with it.

"I'm just an old frump … I haven't had my hair done for six months."

"Your hair looks fine."

"Its not. Look at me. My hair is grey. And my nails broken and chipped." She shows her hands to Helmut. "Why can't I be like them?"

"Don't start, mama". Helmut looks around to see if anyone is watching them. No-one is interested in them at all. "When you're finished your tea we can pop into a hairdressers … get you done up all nice."

Gisela brightens like a child, then appears deflated. "You can't just turn up at a hair salon. You have to book."

"We'll tell them that you have a wedding to go to tomorrow."

"Nobody gets married on a Sunday."

"I'll think of something. Leave it to me." He finishes his tea.

"Muti?" Her tone has softened. "How are we going to pay for the treatment?"

"I always take care of you, don't I?" Helmut gets up, takes his mother's coat, and helps her to put it on.

"Ya. You are full of miracles when it comes to money. My hair might cost fifty pounds or more."

Helmut registers a slight twinge of pain. "I said leave it to me, mama."

*

Helmut exits from a high street hair salon. He turns up the collar of his jacket and joins the throng of Saturday shoppers. He spots a well-dressed affluent young man in his mid-twenties putting his wallet into the inside pocket of his coat. The man is carrying a bag of shopping from a department store and starts to walk towards Helmut.

Helmut puts his head down, walks in a direct line straight towards him. They bump heavily into one another.

"Sorry". Helmut puts his hand on the man's arm in apology, and then walks on.

Helmut is pleased with himself. He has swiped the wallet. He slides it into his own jacket pocket. Then from behind he hears "You clumsy wanker!"

Helmut stops dead in his tracks. He turns slowly. The man he has robbed jerks two fingers up to him. "You watch where you're going the next time, fucker." Helmut returns a weak smile.

The man turns on his heel and disappears into the throng of afternoon shoppers. Helmut takes out the wallet, opens it. Inside are two theatre tickets, a wad of cash, some debit cards, and a driving license. He takes out the driving license, looks at it, and smiles.

"Eric Roehampton …..."

A CCTV camera above him moves. He is aware of the cameras being everywhere. He lowers his head and exits by a side street. As he is walking back to his car, a traffic warden is putting a ticket on his windscreen. Before he gets to his car, the traffic warden crosses the road. Helmut follows him.

The traffic warden goes into a small park. Helmut looks around. There are a few people but they are all going about their own business. The traffic warden disappears behind some laurel bushes. Helmut takes out a pair of tan leather gloves from his jacket pocket, puts them on.

In the shrubbery, the traffic warden is rolling a joint. He is sprinkling cannabis leaf into a rolling paper spread with tobacco. There is a rustle of leaves. The traffic warden turns and looks over his shoulder, shrugs, and carries on rolling his joint. He reaches for his disposable lighter, raises it to the end of his fat cigarette. The paper catches alight. He inhales and as he blows out the smoke, he breaks into a broad grin.

As he puts the joint back to his lips to inhale again, a loop of barbed wire comes over his head and is pulled tight around his throat. The joint drops from his mouth.

Helmut is behind him looping more barbed wire around his throat. The traffic warden drops to his knees choking for air. Helmut has his knee in the small of his back and is pulling with all his strength on the loops of wire. The traffic warden is gurgling, his hands clenching and unclenching as Helmut strangles him.

Helmut now has his foot in the small of the traffic warden's back. He jerks the wire hard – almost decapitates the traffic warden. He lets go of the ends and the traffic warden drops lifeless into the undergrowth.

Helmut looks at his gloves, checks

that they are not damaged. He picks up the traffic warden's ticket machine and scrolls through the entries. He finds a picture of his car. And another. He deletes them. He takes the warden's Casio ticket machine and finds his own registration number. The machine has GPS tracking. He looks unconcerned.

Helmut returns to his Beetle. He opens the front located trunk and takes out a screwdriver from his toolbox and two number plates. He looks around for cameras. He sees none. He closes the trunk. He changes the front and back plates on his car.
Helmut slides into the driver's seat. He throws the handheld ticket machine on to the passenger seat. The GPS flashes. He takes the stolen wallet and opens it. He takes out the driving license. He picks up the handheld and types in the address on the driving license.
A vehicle registration pops up. He smiles. He throws the handheld down again. He turns on the ignition, puts the car in gear, drives

off.

*

A quiet leafy street. Helmut descends a short flight of steps to a basement apartment. He is wearing overalls and has an electric drill in his hand.

He runs his hand along the ledge above the door, finds nothing. He looks under the matt. A Yale key. He picks it up and puts it in the lock. He turns the key - the door opens gently.

Inside the flat there is classical music playing. He recognises it as German. He thinks it is Bach. The place is well furnished, and is arty. It is an obvious bachelor pad but there is a hint of a female touch. There is incense burning.

Helmut admires a framed nude photograph on the wall. There is the sound of laughter over the music. Helmut crosses the living room.

A door is ajar. He looks in. It is the master bedroom. The bed is unmade and there are clothes lying on the floor. Helmut puts his finger on the trigger of the drill. The drill whirls for barely a second. He hears the laughter again.

He goes down the hall towards the kitchen. There is the sound of splashing. He turns from the kitchen to the bathroom. The door is slightly ajar. He pushes the door open a little more. There is condensation on the mirror and walls. He pushes the door open further. It reveals a shower curtain covering the front of a bath. There is water on the floor and towels strewn across the bidet.

Helmut eases his way towards the curtain. The steam is heavy. He is beginning to sweat. He wipes is free hand on his overalls. He flexes his grip on the drill. There is the sound of water slapping the side of the bath.

Helmut reaches for the end of the curtain. The sweat is dripping from his forehead. A female hand is gripping the side of the bath.

"Are you coming, Fifi?"

"Yes. ... do what you want to me!"

He slowly eases back the curtain. Eric Roehampton is humping a blonde from behind. Their backs are to Helmut.

"Are you coming??? Don't lie to me,!"

"Yes, Eric. I'm coming ... I'm coming!"

Helmut's eyes flare. His finger presses on the drill. Eric turns instantly. Helmut pushes the racing drill bit into his forehead. There is a gruesome sound of metal shattering bone. Blood splatters everywhere. The drill stops rotating. It is stuck in Eric's head.

Fifi starts to scream.

Helmut puts the drill into reverse. It whines as it leaves Eric's forehead. A gush if blood spurts out on to Fifi's back as he falls on her, his dead body pinning her in the bath. Her head goes under the water. She thrashes in the blood filled water, kicks to get Eric off her. Her head pops up out of the water. Helmut grabs her by the hair, brutally hauls her out of the bath.

She is screaming and kicking as he pulls her on to the floor. He knocks the wind out of her, drags her towards the toilet bowl, reaches up and grabs the toilet tissue.

Fifi is starting to regain her breath. She opens her mouth to scream. Helmut punches her, knocks the stuffing out of her. He gets on top of her, pins her to the floor with his knees, and stuffs toilet paper into her mouth. She stops struggling. Her eyes watch him as he reaches for the drill lying on the floor.

He takes an Allen-key from his overalls, and starts to change the head on the drill. "Have you had a nice afternoon, Fifi? I'm just here to do a bit of DIY."

Helmut take a long screw from his pocket. Fifi panics, starts to throw her head from side to side as she watches him put the screw on the end of the drill head.

He grabs her left arm, extends it. She resists but doesn't have the strength to fight him. He pins her hand down, and drills through her palm, screws it to the floor. Her fingers wriggle like worms as she convulses and kicks in horror and pain.

He forces her other hand down, screws it to the floor. She is choking on the tissue in her mouth. The pain makes her look as though her eyes are about to pop out of her head. Helmut moves down her body and screws her left foot to the floor. Then her right foot.

He gets up and looks at his handwork. "Very catholic, very martyr like."

He turns back to look at Eric in the bath. "He shouldn't have called me a wanker."

He changes the screw-head back to the drill bit. He drops back on to Fifi, puts his hand on her breast, feels for her heartbeat.

"There it is. Must be doing all of a hundred and twenty." He takes a marker pen from his overalls and puts an x over her heart.

Fifi is beside herself.

Helmut spins the drill head. "You should pick your men more carefully. Nice flat, nice things, but he wasn't nice, was he?" Fifi is shaking her head side to side. "Oh well. Girls will be girls." He moves the drill head on to the x.

Fifi is starting to lose consciousness. With his other hand be removes the paper from her mouth. "Fifi ..." He taps her gently on the head to keep her conscious. "Come on, stay awake. That's my girl. You are very good. So I'm going to be kind to you." He closes her eyelids. "You won't want to see what happens next." He squeezes the drill trigger.

Helmut exits the flat top to toe wearing Eric's clothes and his overcoat. He is carrying two plastic bags. He opens his car, places one of the plastic bags in the back seat, then picks up the handheld ticket machine from the passenger seat.

On the street he glances about looking at the cars. He presses the unlock button of a car key. A BMW beeps. The number plate matches the registration displayed on the handheld. He smiles.

He crosses the street to the BMW and opens the driver's door. He places the handheld on the seat, removes the overalls from the bag and throws them into the back of the car. The drill remains in the bag. He throws the key on to the dashboard and slams the door closed.

He walks slowly back to his own car. He opens the trunk and puts the plastic bag containing the drill into his tool box He gets in and drives off.

*

Helmut enters the hair salon. Gisela is in the final stages of having her nails buffed.

"How much do I owe you?" Helmut asks the girl at the till. She punches some keys "Seventy two pounds."

"No problem." Helmut peels off four twenty-pound notes from Eric's wallet. "Keep the rest as a tip."

The girl smiles warmly. "Thanks."

"You ready, mama?" Gisela looks at him oddly "Where did you get that coat, Muti?"

"You like it? Got it in a charity shop."

Gisela runs her hand down it. "Its lovely. Its mohair? Reminds me of the races." She puts on her hat. "We look a right pair of toffs."

They exit the salon.

Helmut and Gisela are walking down the promenade arm in arm. "Look at my nails. The girls in the salon were very sweet. Do you like my hair?"

"You look a million dollars, mama."

"Oh, you are just humouring your old mother."

"No, mama, you look just lovely."

She stops, takes out a cigarette from her handbag. "All done up but with nowhere to go."

Helmut pulls out the tickets from the wallet. "I got us two tickets for the theatre tonight."

"Really?" She is surprised and excited. "What's the show? Is it Shakespeare?"

"I don't think so. It's called Murder in the House."

"Is that a who dunnit? I quite like who dunnits. I usually work out who the murderer is after about ten minutes. I'm never wrong."

"You should have been a detective, mama."

"I could have been. The police in Deutschland are terrible at solving murders."

He opens the car door for her.

"I'm telling you. All those unsolved murders in Munich. If I had been on it, I would have the caught the killer in a week." Gisela gets into the car.

"You think so?" Helmut closes the passenger door, goes around to the other side of the car and gets in.

"Serial killers are all oddballs. It doesn't take much detective work to spot an oddball."

"If you say so." He is half listening.

"You don't believe me do you, Muti?"

"I never said that, mama."

"You know I have highly developed psychic powers."

"You haven't used them for a long time."

"I'm using them now."

"Have a cigarette, mama."

"Don't dismiss me like that. I'm your mother!"

"Sorry, mama."

"I worry about you, Muti. Did you really get that coat in a charity shop?"

"Yes, mama ….."

Gisela seems relieved. Helmut pops the cigarette lighter, hands it to her. She lights her cigarette. He leans over and picks up the plastic bag from the back seat. "I got you something to wear for the theatre." He pulls an evening dress from the bag. "It's your size, mama."

Gisela looks at the label. She is impressed. "Its gorgeous. Is this from the charity shop too?"

"Of course. Same shop as the coat." Helmut turns the ignition. He looks in the mirror, pulls out.

*

In the room, Helmut is facing the

window. "Can I look now, mama?"

"Nein. I'm not ready, yet."

"We're going to be late."

"Be quite, Helmut! I'm a woman. I need time with these things." Helmut shuffles his feet with impatience. "Damn it!" Gisela swears.

"Are you alright?" Helmut turns to see his mother squeezed into the dress he has acquired for her. It is obvious that it belonged to a younger woman like Fifi. Gisela is spilling out of it.

"Zip me up, son." Helmut forces the zip all the way up to the top of the dress. "I can hardly breathe."

"You look great, mama."

"Get me my coat before I pass out." Helmut does as he is told, collects the coat from a peg. He slips his mother's old coat over her shoulders. She tries to put an arm into a sleeve, but Helmut prevents her. "Looks better draped over your shoulders like that."

"I'll get cold dressed like this!"

"We'll get a taxi to the theatre."

"I don't know how we are affording all this."

"I told you before. Leave all the

money worries to me." He opens the door to the landing. "Ready?" he hands Gisela's handbag to her. Gisela gives him a look. "Please, mama, be nice to me."

"I'm always nice to you, Helmut." She passes through the door.

Helmut face registers his love and hate for his mother in the same expression. He closes the door.

*

Three players are on the stage. It is a Victorian melodrama. Helmut and Gisela are seated near the back of the theatre. Gisela points to one of the players. "That's the murderer."

"Shoosh, mama."

"Don't shoosh me. That's the one, I'm telling you."

"Will you be quiet?" A middle-aged man directly in front of Gisela is glaring at her. He turns to face the front again. Gisela kicks the man's seat. "I beg you pardon!" The man is irate.

"Be quiet, you oaf!" Gisela kicks his seat again. The man does not want to cause any further trouble. He turns back to watch the play. Gisela gives Helmut a big smile. Helmut slides down into his chair in embarrassment.

Outside on the steps of the theatre, Gisela is sucking deeply on a fag. Helmut is playing with the lighter he acquired from Colin. "Ach, Helmut, put it away … you are worse than your father."

"I don't think that is possible."

Gisela suddenly pulls the fag from her lips. "There he is."

"Who?" Helmut turns to see the middle-aged man and his wife leaving the theatre.

"Go and have a word with him, Muti. He was so rude to me!"

Helmut smiles. "Mama, you can be so melodramatic. You were rude to him."

Gisela stubs out her cigarette with the heel of her shoe. "I never get any support from you. I'm getting old and I can see that you'd be happy for me to be put in a home." Gisela wraps her coat tightly around herself and descends the stairs.

"Mama!" Helmut is wounded by his mother's accusation. He catches up with her. "I can't stand it when you say such things."

"It's because it's true. You think I

am a burden on you. You get only one mother in life. I don't know why you are so cruel to me. Other people's sons don't treat their mothers with the indifference you have for me. You betray me at every possible turn. You are a wicked, nasty boy!" She strikes him hard across the face with the palm of her hand.

Helmut does not react. His eyes are motionless, dead and distant as his mother hits him again across his face, this time with the back of her hand. "See, what you make me do! You make me so angry! Why can't you just be nice to your old mama?" She stares at him.

Helmut lowers his head in shame. "I'm sorry ..."

Her expression softens. She takes his face in his hands. "I know you are ..." She pulls him into her bosom as if he is a little boy. Helmut sheds a tear.

"I love you, mama. I didn't mean to hurt you."

"Quiet now, Muti." She strokes his hair. "It was all that man's fault. It is always the same, liebschen. We try to enjoy ourselves but these kinds of people just won't accept us. They think we are scum because we are foreign. What use are good clothes if they can't hide the kind of people we are."

"What are we, mama?"

"Special, Helmut. We are very special people. Nobody knows how special we are. They can turn their noses up at us, but we are God's chosen ones. It is our secret." She lifts Helmut's head and kisses him on the lips. "There. Alles besser." She wipes the lipstick from his lips with her thumb. "Kommen sie." She loops her arm into his.

They begin to walk down the pavement towards their car. "I was right, leibchen" she says matter of fact like.

"About what, mama?"

"The murderer. I worked it out in the first ten minutes."

3

Back in their small bed-sit, Gisela is fast asleep on her bed in the window alcove. Helmut is restlessly tossing and turning in his sleep. He awakes. He listens. There is a SOUND from the street. Voices.

Gisela stirs. "Muti. I can't sleep with that noise."

Helmut gets up, pulls back the net curtain and sees below three youths, cans of beer in their hands, staggering about the street. His eyes narrow. "It's alright, mama. I'll go and ask them to keep it down."

The three youths, Gary, Hanson and Izzy, are out of their faces from consuming too much alcohol. Gary is pissing up against a wall. Izzy is holding up Hanson who is trying to kiss her. She is not enjoying the attention. "You got any booze at your place?" she asks Gary.

Hanson is still trying to kiss her on the neck.

"I got half a bottle of vodka."

"Is that all?" She is struggling to straighten Hanson up "God sake, Hanson, man!"

"I got some weed." Gary puts his prick away, lifts his can of beer perched on the wall, and staggers over to Izzy and Hanson. He puts his hand on Hanson's shoulder. "You make it to my gaff, man?"

Hanson tries to straighten "I'm a bit

pissed. Which way is it?"
Gary takes advantage of Hanson's disorientation. He puts his arm around Izzy's skinny waist and kisses her. Izzy responds to Gary's advances. His hands wander down to her hemline and start to push up into her underwear.
"Fuck me, Izzy. What you doing?" Hanson complaints.
She looks at Hanson, taunts him. "You want to fuck me, Gary? He's too pissed."
Hanson forces them apart. "That's enough. You're my girlfriend!"
"No I'm not!" Izzy pushes Hanson off.
Gary apologies to Hanson. "Sorry, mate. Got carried away." He swigs on his can, empties the contents. He squeezes the can, screws it up. With a show of his prowess to Izzy, he lobs the can far into the dark. The can lands with a clunk and a scrape at the feet of Helmut.

The three youths are now in a small narrow cutting. Hanson is doubled over being sick while Gary and Izzy are eyeing one another up.
"You like my mate?" Gary asks.

"Don't know," Izzy shrugs.

"You must know if you like him?"

"He's alright. Bit of a tosser sometimes."

"You're his first girlfriend. You gonna break his heart?"

"I'm not his girlfriend. I've only known him three weeks."

"Same as me, right?" Gary pulls her to him, pushes his other hand down the front of her skirt. He fumbles about.

"You know what you're looking for?" she teases him.

"Yeah. I know wot girls like." Gary finds her spot.

She gasps a little, goes short of breath. "How do I know you don't just want me because I'm with your mate?"

"Cause I was watching you when you woz dancing?"

"Snap. I was watching you watching me." Their passion is beginning to spill over. She puts her hand down the front of his jeans.

Hanson straightens up.

"I feel like shit." He turns towards his friends. Izzy pushes Gary away and smooths down her skirt. Gary rearranges his flies.

"You'll be alright in the morning."
She goes to him, wipes some sick
from his face.

"I really like you, Izzy."

"Yeah, you plonker. I know you do.
Come on." She puts her arm around
him, starts to lead him along the
cutting. Gary is leading the way.

"You got a hot one there, Hanson.
Don't you fuck it up with her, mate.
She's alright. Fuck!" Something has
hit him on the cheek. It bounces on
to the path. It is the beer can he
tossed away earlier.

"Who the fuck did that!" he shouts
in a rage. He feels his cheek. There
is blood oozing from the gash.

"Did what?" asks Izzy unaware of
what has happened. Helmut appears
from the dark. His hands are behind
his back.

"Who the fuck are you?" Gary is
livid. He kicks the can at Helmut.
"Did you chuck that at me?"

Helmut steps forward, smiles. "You
woke my mother up. You should
learn some manners."

"Are you taking the piss? We're
doing nothing wrong. It's Saturday
night. We can do what the fuck we
want. It's a free world."

"How old are you?"

"Nineteen."

Hanson staggers forward "Who's this guy?" He is trying to focus. "Are you a policeman?"

"You're going to wish I was."

Gary stiffens, ready to fight. Hanson appeals to Helmut. "Cmon, mister, we're just having some fun. We're sorry we woke up your mum."

Helmut addresses Izzy "You sorry too?"

Izzy doesn't want any trouble. "Yes, sorry. We were a bit noisy back there. We're sorry aren't we, Gary?"

Gary weighs the situation, relaxes. "Yeah, sorry, mate."

Helmut steps towards Gary, stops a few feet from him. "I'm glad I'm your mate, Gary. I've been watching you, sticking your fingers into Izzy's cunt. When I was nineteen, a prick like you beat the shit out of me for looking at his girlfriend. What if I was to stick my fingers into Izzy's cunt. Would you mind, Hanson? Or would you beat the shit out of me, Gary?"

Hanson is frightened. "How's he know our names?"

"Well, Izzy? You want to be fucked

by me?"

"Fuck off! You're gross!" Izzy tucks herself in behind Gary. Helmut slowly brings his gloved hands from behind his back.

"I don't take rejection well." In a fluid movement, he pulls his Samurai sword from its sheathe and decapitates Gary. As Gary's torso falls, a second stroke decapitates Izzy. Hanson stands paralysed, in a complete state of shock.

"She was two timing you, mate. Don't feel sorry for her. Feel sorry for yourself." Helmut smiles "I'm putting you out of your misery." He thrusts the blade into Hanson's belly nearly up to the hilt. He places Hanson's hands on the handle. "The Japanese call it Sora. You'll see it when they open the gates." Helmut pushes the last of blade hard into Hanson's stomach.

It is all over in a matter of seconds. He watches and waits for Hanson to fall to the ground, the sword blade protruding out of his back.

Helmut removes Hanson's red-sneakers, places them on his own feet. They are a perfect fit. He puts his own discarded shoes picked up at Eric's flat on the dead teenager's feet.

*

It is early morning. Gisela is sitting in her dressing gown looking at herself in a small hand mirror. She is obsessed by her wrinkles and is pulling her skin back behind her ears to look younger. Helmut stirs in his bed.

"I need plastic surgery." She looks over to her son whose eyes are still closed. "Did you hear me, Helmut?"

Helmut opens his eyes.

"No, mama?"

"I need plastic surgery."

Helmut keeps his eyes closed. "No, mama. I think you are beautiful the way you are."

"You have your eyes closed! Look at me! Tell me I need plastic surgery."

Helmut opens his eyes. He has a look of exasperation as he turns towards his mother.

"You don't need plastic surgery."

Gisela does not accept the answer. "Come over here. Look. Every part of my face is wrinkled like an old hag."

Helmut gets up. He is naked.

"Helmut! You know I don't like to see any man naked! Put on some clothes!" Helmut wraps a towel around his midriff, puts on the red-sneakers.

"You're in a bad mood this morning, mama."

"It's Sunday. You know that every Sunday I like to read the papers mit ein kleine tasse espresso."

"Ja, mama."

"Come, Muti, see ..." she shows him her face in the light. "Can you see how this life has made me old before my time? Feel my skin." Helmut puts his hand on his mother's face. She places her hand over his. "Its like the face of a crocodile."

"No it's not. Your skin is lovely and smooth."

"You can't flatter me. You're my son. The truth, now. Bitte!" Helmut is wary that the wrong answer will bring on his mother's wrath.

"No, really, mama, you are in marvellous condition for your age. I don't know any other sixty year old with such beautiful skin."

She draws away angrily. "I am not sixty!"

"Of course you are."

"That's not what my passport says".
She picks up her passport. "It says
that I am fifty one!"

"That is not your real passport. You
are not Frances Butcher,
remember."

Gisela breaks into tears. "What a
sham life we have. Because of you!"

"Don't mama!"

"I regret the day you were born.
You gave me so much pain I never
wanted to have a child again! Now,
you pain me even more. You are the
cruellest son a mother ever had."

Helmut is not giving into her
hysterics this time. "Look. I'll get
dressed and go out and buy the
Sunday papers." Gisela stops crying.
"I'll get you a double espresso as
well."

Gisela looks up. "So you don't think
I need plastic surgery?"

"Even if you did, how would we
afford it?"

"So you think I need surgery."

"Mama! Drop this please."

Gislea picks up the mirror again,
examines herself. "Perhaps a little
botox? That is not expensive, right?"

"I don't know." Helmut is not

listening. He has hurriedly dressed and is preparing to leave. Gisela lights a cigarette. "Do you need more cigarettes, mama?"

"Nein, Muti, danke." She raises a half full packet.

Helmut nods, departs.

*

Helmut is returning along the street with the Sunday papers in a plastic bag, and two take-away coffees. As he passes a lamppost, he sees a yellow ribbon tied around it. He stops. There is a poster taped to the post.

MISSING – Brenda Mackie.

Helmut recognises the picture of the sixteen year old he has murdered. He looks up and down the street. People are going about their business. He walks on a little, comes to another lamppost with a yellow ribbon.

MISSING – Brenda Mackie

As he rounds the corner into the street of the boarding house, he sees that all the lampposts have yellow ribbons tied around them and missing posters of Brenda. A passer-by with a dog stops and comments,

"They'll never find her."

Helmut is surprised at the statement. "Why's that?"

"Girls go missing all the time in this country. They find one in twenty."

"Do you know anything about this Brenda?" Helmut asks.

"God knows. People say she was a lovely girl. Bright. Intelligent. Thought that she might even try for Oxford."

"What a shame." Helmut tries generate some empathy without sounding hollow.

"Its always the lovely ones that get themselves into trouble. There's a few toe-rags around here I wouldn't miss in a month of Sundays. Nice meeting you."

"Yes, you too."

The passer-by walks on, his dog taking a backward glance at Helmut. Helmut shudders a little. He looks at the picture as if he doesn't remember the girl, feels sorry for her.

Gisela, wearing her spectacles, is happily reading the newspaper and sipping the last of her coffee. Helmut is lying on his bed reading the property guide section.

"Muti. Remember we went to the pier yesterday?"

"Yes, mama …."

"Two young people were found drowned under the pier."

Helmut stops reading, continues to stare at the guide. "Really?"

"They've been identified as Colin Mercer and Doreen Middleton. Isn't that the same name as that princess? I wonder if it's the same family."

"It's a common enough name." Helmut is trying to remain disinterested.

"You never know. Oh it's sad. They committed suicide. Eighteen years old. What a waste." She takes off her glasses. "I think we should find a chapel and say a prayer for them."

Helmut closes the property guide.

"Don't be angry with me, Muti. I know I am sentimental and filled with foolish sympathises for the poor starving children in Africa, but what if we had been on the pier and seen that young couple? We could have stopped them, talked some common sense into them." She is up on her feet and reaching for her coat.

"I must say a prayer for them. I must. It is my duty. I can only imagine how their mothers must be feeling at this very moment. It's a tragedy. A senseless tragedy." Helmut is angry.

"Mama! Stop it! You are making yourself hysterical." Gisela reacts slowly to her son's accusation.

"I am rational and calm. I am thinking only of the need to show some respect for the dead. Now, as my son, I want you to drive me to the nearest chapel so that I can pray. It is a Sunday, and that is what good Christian mothers do. They go to chapel."

Helmut has no answer to his mother's reasoning. In defeat, he rises and reaches for his new coat.

Gisela smiles. "That's my boy. I remember the first time I took you to Sunday school. You did not want me to leave you with the other children. You had quiet a ball and shout, but I was firm. I always have to be firm with you. It is for your own good." She puts her hand on his forearm. "Now, come, let's make our peace with God and then find a

lovely place to take lunch."
Helmut opens the door, follows his mother out.

Helmut and Gisela are in the car as it pulls out of parking and starts along the street. Through the windscreen, they see ahead a police cordon tape stretched across the road. A Policeman is plainly visible standing in the middle of the road. Helmut stops the car, winds down his side window.
The Policeman steps forward. "Sorry, sir, but you will have to turn around."
"What's doing on?"
"I can't tell you that."
"We live in this street. We have a right to know?"
The Policeman looks into the car, sees Gisela, smiles to her. "Did you hear any disturbance last night?"
"No" Helmut quickly answers.
Gisela looks at him, "But Helmut, don't you remember. There was some shouting in the street. It woke me up."
"You are a light sleeper, mama." He confides in the Policeman "There was some noise, but this street is

always like that when the pubs come out." He leans out the window, whispers. "Please tell me why we can't drive thorough. My mother will worry otherwise."

The Policemen softens, feels relieved to be giving out the information. "Three young persons have been found dead."

"In the street?"

"Down the alleyway."

"What's he saying, Muti?"

"I'm asking him where the nearest chapel is."

The Policeman takes his cue. "Yes, if you turn around, and take the left at the main road, about a mile along you'll see St. Magdeline's."

"Thank you." Helmut three point turns the car, watches the Policeman recede in his wing mirror. Gislea has her head in her hands.

"Are you okay, mama?"

"No, I'm not." She turns to look at him. "Why do these things always happen when we find somewhere new to live?"

"What do you mean?"

"Don't try to hide it from me. Someone has been killed? Why else would they spend the money to have a policeman stop cars?"

Helmut tries to find a reasonable counter-argument. "Yes, someone has been killed. That's not unusual. The world is a violent place. You watch American cop shows? People get killed all the time. Fifty in every million."

"Not in England."

"Yes, mama, in England too. There are twelve murders per million people. In Germany it is only eight."

"How do you know such things, Helmut?"

"I've got a good memory for figures."

"Its morbid figures. Morbid!"

Helmut leads Gisela into a chapel. She crosses herself. The chapel has only a few worshippers in the pews. "We've missed the service, mama."

"I don't need a priest to help me to pray." She throws off Helmut's arm and goes forward down the aisle. Helmut watches as she settles in the front pew. He is uncomfortable at being in the chapel. The statues frighten him, make him anxious. He pushes himself against the chapel wall, feels for the safety of an alcove.

As he settles on a chair, his attention is drawn to the confession box. A beautiful girl about twenty years old, pushes quickly out of the left side of the confession box. She looks upset. Almost immediately, the right side opens and a young priest not much older than the girl snatches hold of the girl's wrist. The priest draws the girl to him, but she struggles, shakes free of his grip.

"No, Jacamo! It is not right."

"I love you, Karin."

"No." The girl is close to tears. "I'm not going to have the baby. I want to finish my studies."

"You will murder my child? God will never forgive you!"

This last statement is too much for Karin. She breaks free and rushes out of the chapel. Jacamo sinks back into the confession box seat, pulls close the curtain. Helmut gets up approaches the confessional.

There is the sound of sobbing.

Helmut enters the left side of the box, closes the curtain. The sobbing stops. There is a moment of silence. Then the sound of Jacamo blowing his nose.

"Father" Helmut whispers.

There is a delay, then a response.

"Yes, can I help you?"

"Yes, father. I have sinned."

"We are all sinners in the eyes of the Lord."

"I'm a murderer, father?"

There is a pause. "Have you lost a child?"

"No, I have taken many lives ..."

"What is your profession, my son?"

 "I am a butcher, father."

There is a sigh of relief. "There is nothing wrong with taking the lives of God's creatures. The Lord said 'Eat anything that is sold in the marketplace without question of conscience. Everything that is sold at the butcher's shop you may eat without inquiry.'"

"Then I am forgiven?" Helmut removes his belt from his trousers.

"There is nothing to forgive, my son." He slides open the dividing hatch. "Are you new to our parish?"

Helmut looks the priest in the eye. "Yes, father. Can I ask you a question?"

"Please ….."

He loops the end of the belt through the buckle. "Are priests allowed to have children?" Jacamo is suspicious of the question.

"Why do you ask?" Helmut swifty drops the belt over the priest's head and jerks on it so hard, Jacamo's head is pulled through the hatch. Jacomo's eyes begin to bulge as he chokes.

"Let's hear your confession then, father." Helmut tugs on the belt. "Come on. Own up about the girl."

"I am sorry. I have truly sinned. Oh, I am so ashamed."

"I forgive you." Helmut pulls tighter on the belt. "Let's hear the Apostles Creed."

"No, no" Jacamo realises he is about to die.

Helmut is insistent. "You want to go to heaven?"

Jacamo cries a little, starts slowly "I believe in God, the Father almighty ..."

Helmut pulls on the belt. "Quicker!"

Jacamo quickens "... creator of heaven and earth. I believe in the Holy Spirit, the holy catholic church, the communion of saints, the forgiveness of sins, the resurrection of the body, and life everlasting. Amen"

"Amen." Helmut takes a slice of chewing gum and places it in Jacamo's mouth "This is the Lamb of God who takes away the sins of the world. Happy are those called to his supper." He slackens the belt. "Are you happy?"

"Lord I am not worthy to receive you, but only say the word and I shall be healed."

Helmut whispers "The Body of Christ."

Jacamo cries "Amen."

Helmut tightens the belt "May the Lord Jesus protect you and lead you to eternal life."

Jacamo's feet are kicking against the wooden walls of the confessional. Gisela, disturbed from her prayers, looks up. Jacamo's life is draining from him. His kicking stops. Gisela goes back to her prayers.

Helmut hauls on the belt, ties the loose end around the top of the confessional framework to make it look as though Jacamo has hung himself. Jacamo jangles, twitches. Helmut removes the cross that dangles from Jacamo's neck. He slips out of the confessional, and advances by two hours the hands of the cardboard clock that marks the time until the next confessional session.

Helmut is sitting on the steps of the chapel picking at a caked spot of blood on his red sneakers. Gisela emerges. "You go to confession, mama?"
"I've nothing to confess, Muti. My conscience is clear. I wish you would take the faith, son. Your atheist father is to blame. Putting into your head all those communist ideas that workers should rule the world. Workers, pah! Busy hands, idle heads."
"Have a cigarette, mama,"
Gisela lights up, takes a deep draw.
"I would like to go for a drive."
"What about lunch?"
"We can have a picnic. Drink champagne."
Helmut is exasperated, lets out a long sigh.

*

Helmut is carrying a wire shopping basket around a supermarket. He has filled the basket with meats, cheeses and a bottle of champagne. He is making his way to the bread stand. As he reaches for a French stick, a can of tuna rolls across the floor. He stoops to pick it up.

"Sorry" a timid female voice says.

Helmut, with the can in his hand, looks up. It is Karin from the chapel. He is completely smitten by her beauty.

"I'm not myself today."

Helmut hands her the can. He feels awkward and shy.

"Thank you." She looks down at his basket. "You are celebrating?"

"No, nothing special."

"I've never drunk champagne."

"It really is nothing special."

"Then why does everyone drink it on special occasions?"

"I don't know. Good marketing perhaps?"

She laughs innocently. Helmut stares at her with total fascination.

"What's your name? I'm Karin."

"Bob …. "

"Are you from Brighton, Bob?"

"No, I'm from all over really. English, half German. Where are you from?"

"Ukraine."

"That's a long way away. Lots of troubles there, eh?"

"Yes, unfortunately. I'm stuck here in England all on my own."

"No boyfriend?"

"Not really …. I was with a boy but it wasn't right. Have you a girlfriend?"

Helmut blushes "No."

Karin brightens. "Really? I would have thought that as you are very good looking, you …."

"I look after my mother." Helmut is embarrassed.

"That's a nice thing to do. Is she old?"

"Getting on." Helmut seizes his chance. "Would you like to meet her? She's just outside"

Karin starts to make an excuse, then looks at Helmut, gives him a warm smile. "Yes, why not."

"I'm not taking up your time?"

"No, not at all. I'm just wandering about the supermarket as there is not much to do on a Sunday."

In the car park, Gisela has her handbag emptied out on to the bonnet of the car. She has obviously lost something that she cannot find. She rummages in the lining of her bag, produces a half smoked cigarette. She sticks it behind her ear and refills her handbag. Helmut, carrying the shopping, approaches with Karin. "Mama, this is Karin from Kiev."

Gisela's eyes narrow, then dilate as she puts on her best manners. "Kiev. My father fought the Russians there during the war. Lovely to meet you"

"It's my pleasure to meet you. Bob thinks the world of you."

Gisela approves of Karin's manners. "How sweet of you to say." She turns to her son. "Is she coming on the picnic with us, Muti?"

"We've just met, mama." Helmut hands his mother a fresh pack of cigarettes.

"She is a lovely girl. You must come with us on our picnic."

"I would be in the way?" Karen offers meekly.

"Not at all. We would enjoy the company."

Helmut is uncertain. "Mama. Karin has her studies."

"Nonsense. Coming with us will be an education. We are very special." She takes Karin by the hands. "You are my guest."

Karin seems happy to swept along.
"Where are you having the picnic?"
"On the cliffs along the coast. I read about it. Its called Beachy Head."
She turns to Helmut. "You have the champagne, leibchen?"
"Yes, mama."
The thought of drinking champagne is the clincher for Karin. "I only have a can of tuna to contribute."
"Keep it for the cat, darling" Gisela quips. "Come, let's get in the car. You can sit in the front with my son."
Helmut and Karin lock eyes, exchange shy smiles, get in the car.

The car is travelling along the cliff road that leads beyond Peacehaven. In the car, the party of three are listening to the car radio. Helmut and Karin keep stealing glances at one another. Gisela is happy leaning back smoking a cigarette. She is thoroughly enjoying her day out.

A lighthouse lies below. Helmut, carrying most of the picnic items is leading the way. Gisela has Karin's arm for support.
"I don't have a head for heights.

What about you?" Gisela asks.

"I'm okay with it." Karin looks out "They are very big cliffs."

"Its a favourite spot for suicides. Maybe we'll see someone jump." Gisela laughs. "Sorry, being German I have a very black sense of humour. Don't listen to my foolish thoughts."

"No, its fine. You say what you want."

"You are a lovely girl, Karin."

"I'm not perfect."

Something in Karin's tone makes Gisela stop. "Nobody's perfect, darling." She studies the girl's unhappy face. "Is there something wrong? A secret, eh? All girls have secrets. What's the matter?"

"I'm pregnant."

Gisela laughs. "That's not such a big secret. It will be out soon enough when your belly swells up."

Karin doesn't like that idea. "I want to get rid of it."

"Why?"

"The father is a shit."

Gisela laughs again "That's normal."

Karin is not comforted by Gisela's outburst. She regrets telling her.

"Listen" Gisela adds "Whoever he is,

I can tell he doesn't love you, or you would not be here with me." Karin nods.

Helmut is spreading a blanket on the ground. He straightens and beams proudly at Karin. "Its got to be one of the best views in England!"

"Its just sea, Helmut." Gisela sits on the blanket. Karin joins her.

"Yes, mama, but look how beautiful it looks."

"Hitler didn't think so."

"Hitler?" Helmut asks "What's he got to do with the view?"

Gisela winks at Karin. "If he had conquered England, he would have pulled these cliffs down."

"What?"

"Open the champagne, Muti." She is enjoying winding-up her son. Helmut does as he is told, starts to break the seal on the bottle.

"Why do you call him Muti?" Karen asks.

"Short for Helmut."

"His name is Bob?"

"Its what he's called in England. His middle name. After his grandfather, Robert Butcher." Gisela is playing along with the story they have invented for themselves. Helmut is listening intently.

"Butcher's an odd name?"

"Taylor, Baker, Butcher. Old English name. In German its Fleischer. Just as horrible" she declares. "My maiden name was Razor." Gisela puts on airs and graces. "A very old French name ... very old family."

"My last name is Flyt."

"Flit ...." Gisela draws the name out. "Karin Flit. A very nice name. You wouldn't want Butcher!"

They both laugh.

Helmut pops the cork on the champagne.

"Champagne!" Gisela is an excited teenager again. She pushes some glasses out to Helmut who fills them. She hands Karin a glass. Karin looks at the bubbly and is equally excited.

"This is so wonderful. Drinking champagne with a French aristocrat!"

"Darlings!" Gisela toasts Karin and Helmut.

They drink. Gisela downs hers in one long sip. She encourages Karin to do the same.

"Fill us up, Muti!"

"Mama, you are drinking too fast."

"When I was young, Helmut, I could drink any man under the table." He refills Gisela and Karin's glasses. "Here's to Karin's baby!" Karin is stunned that Gisela has revealed her secret to Helmut. Helmut is stunned too. He stares at Karin.

"You are going to have your baby?"

"Silly boy. What do you mean by that? She's going to have a baby, aren't you darling, and keep it?"

Karin shifts awkwardly. She has no intention of keeping it. Helmut's eyes narrow. He thinks back to the chapel. His mood changes.

"Unwrap the food, Helmut."

Helmut, as usual does as he is told.

"This is a nice spot, Bob .... or should I call you ..."

"Bob" says Helmut matter of factly. "What's Ukraine like, Karin? Compared to England?"

"Very nice." She catches herself. "I mean, its different. The Russians are a problem, but then England has problems too."

"The English themselves." Gisela interjects. "All they want to do is get drunk. Except my boy."

Karin smiles at Helmut. "Do you

think of yourself as English, Bob? Which football team do you support when England plays Germany?"

"He supports Germany, of course!" Gisela declares.

Helmut says nothing.

The picnic has been consumed. Gisela is asleep on the blanket. Helmut and Karin are strolling along the top of the cliff. There is no-one about.

"Have I offended you, Bob?"

"What makes you think that?"

"You don't like me now that you know I'm pregnant?"

"That's not true."

"I can tell. You won't look me in the eye. What if I told you who the father is?"

"I already know."

Karin is puzzled. "You know Jacamo?"

"I found this picture in your handbag." He shows her a photograph of the priest.

Karen is upset. "You went into my handbag?"

He throws the photograph over the cliff. "I also found this." He holds up a nude photograph of her.

She is defensive, "That's not what you think it is. I do modelling to pay my tuition fees."

"That's what you say." He throws it over the cliff.

"What are you doing?"

"Ridding you of your past."

"You don't know me." Karin realises that they are on the edge of the cliff and that Helmut is acting strange. He grabs her by the waist.

"Be careful. It's a long way down. You wouldn't want to commit suicide."

She tries to back away from the edge, but Helmut has her firmly gripped around the waist. Helmut pulls her into him. "When I first saw you, I thought, maybe you could be my girlfriend, someone I could tell everything to, no holding back on secrets. What did you think?"

"I thought," she is careful with her words, "that you looked lonely, like me. It must be a strain looking after your mother?"

"I hate my mother" he snaps.

"She means well ….."

"She hates me."

"No, not at all. Its obvious she loves you."

"She mocks me all the time."

"It's her sense of humour."

"Germans have no humour."

Karin puts her hands on Helmut's hands on her waist. "Thank god the English do. Can we step back from the edge, please? I'm scared."

He lets his arms fall away, turns and looks into her eyes. "You are very beautiful."

Karin faces him, smiles "Thank you. Sorry, the champagne has gone to my head. Just for a moment I thought you were going to push me over." She laughs in relief.

"Do you forgive me for throwing the photographs away?"

"Yes. I understand."

"You don't have to worry about other men." Karin states into Helmut's eyes, sees something evil in them.

"You really want your baby to die?" he asks her

"Yes ….."

"Do you want to die?"

"No … What a silly question."

Helmut is confused. "Why should you live and the baby die?"

He edges her back towards the cliff. She looks over her shoulder. "This is not funny, Bob."

Helmut takes Jacamo's cross from his pocket, forces it into her hand. Her eyes open wide as she realises it is Jacamo's cross. "Say your prayers for the little one." He pushes her hard, and she goes over the edge of the cliff.

He turns away quickly. Suddenly he has an afterthought, halts. He steps back to the cliff's edge and looks over. He is frantic. He realises what he has done. He is consumed by remorse. His mind is racing. He notices Karin's handbag at his feet. He picks up the handbag, empties the contents out on to the grass. He picks through the items, pockets her cellphone, finds a set of house keys. He rummages the contents of the handbag again, this time picks out a utility bill with Karin's name and address on it. He stuffs it in his pocket with the keys.

Gisela wakes up. She is disorientated, and snorts and grunts as she realises where she is. Helmut is sitting beside her. The picnic is packed away and everything is ready to go.

"How long was I asleep?"

"An hour and a half?"

She sits up "I hate waking in the afternoon. It is the only time I get that empty feeling, that there is no point to life." She puts her hand on Helmut's hand. "But you are here, leibchen. You are my life." Helmut smiles, says nothing. "Where is Karin?" she asks.

"She had to go back to Brighton. She got a call from a friend."

"How did she get back?"

"I drove her to the bus stop."

"Is there a bus to Brighton from here?"

"Yes, mama" he says getting up. "I didn't want to wake you. I know how little sleep you get. She asked me to thank you for a lovely afternoon."

Gisela gets up. "I hope she is alright, Helmut. She was very unhappy. Did she give you her phone number."

"Yes, mama."

"Good, boy. I will give her a call later to make sure everything is well with her."

"You fuss too much, mama."

"There are too many people in this

81

world who don't care for anyone but themselves. People need to look out for one another." Helmut lifts the blanket and folds it. "I would love to have a daughter in law like Karin. Perhaps I could match make you two?"

"I don't think she liked me."

"Of course she did. I could she her stealing looks at you all the time. So what if she is going to have another man's baby, it is just biology. What matters is companionship. You need to be think about that. I'm not going to be here forever."

Helmut takes his Mother's arm and leads her back towards the car.

4

Gisela is watching a church service on television. Helmut is in his vest and underpants on his bed reading the sports pages of the Sunday paper he bought in the morning. There is a knock on the door. Gisela does not hear the knocking because of the church service singing.

Helmut gets up, goes to the door, and apprehensively opens it. It is the landlady, a forty-year old widow. She is wearing a kimono dressing gown, a low cut silk slip, and little else.

"Ah, Mister Butcher. I came earlier to see if you were going to be staying on?"

Helmut steps out onto the landing and pulls the door closed behind him. "I'm not sure, Missus Hackett."

"Call me Loretta." She eyes him up. She likes what she sees. "You take your time to decide, Mister Butcher."

Helmut snatches a look at her breasts. "Call me Bob."

"Bob" she repeats. "My dead hubby was called Bob. You look like a handy man to have around. Do you know anything about washing machines?"

"A little bit …."

"I've got a leak from the back of mine. Could you have a look for me?"

"Yes. Just give me a moment to get my tools."

"I'll be downstairs in my kitchen." She slowly turns, winks at Helmut, and starts down the stairs.

Helmut goes back inside.

"Who was that, liebchen?"

He is putting on his trousers. "The landlady." He picks up his toolbox. "She has a small plumbing problem."

"Ask her for a rent reduction for helping her." Helmut half nods. Exits.

Helmut is flat on his back looking behind the washing machine. Loretta is sitting at the kitchen table looking at his athletic stomach and legs.

"My Bob died four years ago. Cancer of the bowel. He kept complaining it was my food but he wouldn't go to the doctor. When he did go, it was too late."

"I'm sorry to hear that."

"Well, life throws us some rotten luck. Bob looked after me though. He was well insured. His payout meant I could buy this place and run it as a boarding house. You've no idea the sort people I've had through here. Sailors, engineers, salesmen, gangsters …."

"Murderers" Helmut adds.

She laughs. "Not as far as I know! God, maybe I have and just don't know it."

Helmut slides out from behind the washing machine. "There we go, all done. Loose drainage hose."

"You're a marvel, Bob." She takes a bottle of wine off a shelf. "Let's have a drink to celebrate."

"Celebrate what?"

"You fixing my washing machine!" She unscrews the cap and starts to pour two very large glasses of white wine. "There you are. Your health, Bob." She clinks his glass, sips from her own, and smiles.

Helmut smiles back. "You got a man, Loretta?"

"I got a few gentlemen callers so to speak, but nobody special."

"And you such a good looking woman."

"You think so. I've had better days, Bob. Much better days. I was quite a looker when I was younger."

"I can see that."

"Well, its life isn't it. It catches up with you. The wine, the late nights, you know …." She puts down her glass. "You want something to eat, Bob?" She opens the fridge door pulls out a large pie. "Here's one I made earlier." She laughs. "I'm a very good cook. I went to cookery school. Proper stuff. Look at that crust. That's professional."

Helmut looks at the pie and nods approvingly.

"I can't stand those cookery shows on telly. The only one I like is Keith Floyd and he died years ago. Didn't matter what it was he cooked, in went the wine! That's my kind of fella." She is cutting the pie with a large kitchen knife.

"Get yourself a plate, Bob." She points to a sideboard. "Every time I cut a pie I think of four and twenty blackbirds." She laughs at herself. Places a large piece of pie on Helmut's plate.

"What is it, Loretta?"

"Its Sweeney Todd pie."

"What's that then?"

"You've led a sheltered life, Bob. Its the leftovers of my tenants." Helmut looks at her in disbelief. "Cor blimey! You're the first one ever to believe me!" She laughs loudly. "Its cherry pie. You want some cream with it?" She pours cream on to his pie.

"I had you going there." She tops his wine up. "I got a wicked sense of humour, I have. You want to see my tits?"

"Sorry …."

"My tit bits. My recipes." She pulls out a large scrapbook. "These are all the recipes I've gathered from tenants. They've come from all over the world. See." Helmut flips the pages. "You got a recipe for me, Bob?"

"I'm not a very good cook."

"Everybody's got one dish to share." Her breasts are falling out of her kimono. Helmut is getting aroused. Loretta knows it.

"I'll ask my mother."

"That's a very small room to be sharing with your mother. Follow me, I'll show you my bedroom."

Helmut follows Loretta out of the kitchen, along the corridor and into her bedroom. It is beautiful decorated in silk and has a four poster bed.

"Try that bed, Bob. Go on, get your lovely bones on there."

Helmut takes off his shoes and climbs on to the bed, lies down. Loretta gets in on the other side and lies beside him.

"You want to see something I look at every night?" Helmut turns and looks at her. She switches on a side-light. "Look up ….."

On the wooden boards topping the four poster are a series of paintings of couples having coitus. "These are some of the positions from the Karma Sutra. How many have you done?"

Helmut's eyes wander over the numerous depictions. Loretta gently unzips his fly and puts her hand into his trousers. Helmut does not resist.

"Maybe two …. three …. two and half."

He is becoming aroused. She takes his hand and puts it on her breast. "Which one would you like to try with me?"

"Do they have numbers?"

She giggles "Bob …. let's start with number one." She pulls him over on top of her.

It is dark outside. Helmut is sitting up in the bed. Loretta enters with a tray of food and places it front of him. "There we are, sweetheart. You need to get your strength back."

"I feel guilty, Loretta. You are spoiling me."

"Why not? You did me a good turn

…. well, a few good turns" she laughs.

"My mother will be wondering what happened to me."

"You got laid, Bob. That's what happened. Eat up, and then I'll send you home to mummy."

"Don't mock me, please."

"Sorry. You're quite a sensitive boy. Why don't you see how your mum is doing and then come back down latter?"

"I can't …."

She slips her hand under the cover and takes hold of his manhood. "Of course you can. You're a grown up." She lets go. "Now, eat up. I want you nice and strong to try that one." She points up.

Helmut laughs.

Helmut returns to the room. Gisela is brooding by the window. "Where have you been?"

"Downstairs talking to Missus Hackett."

"For three hours? You are hardly the world's most talkative person, Helmut."

"Leave me alone, mama. Let me be happy."

"Happy???? What about my happiness? I was left all alone in this awful room. I was worried sick that something had happened to you."

"I was only downstairs."

"That woman is a dog" she utters.

"Mama! Loretta is a very nice person."

"Loretta? You wouldn't know nice from nasty if it licked you or bit you." Gisela sniffs the air. "You stink of perfume. Cheap perfume."

"I'm not listening to you. I'm my own person, and I won't be lectured by you any more."

"Ah so. Now we have it out of you. You want rid of me, you want to replace me with the bitch downstairs."

"Stop it! Stop it!" Helmut has his hands over his ears and is stamping his feet like a little boy.

Gisela moves slowly towards him, speaks in a soft voice. "Liebchen. What is the matter. Tell mama."

Helmut holds up the palm of his right hand. "Don't come near me. I told you to leave me alone. I won't be responsible for what I do."

"What are you going to do?" She is taunting him. "Are you going to pee yourself like you used to? No? Are you going to cry? No, you are a man now. What are you going to do, Helmut? Tell me. What are you going to do?" Helmut remains silent, his head lowered.

Gisela lights a cigarette. "You are going to do what you always do. Nothing. Nothing at all, because you are a little coward who can't even stand up to his frail mother. You are pathetic. How did I end up with a child like you?" She throws a cushion at him. "You deserved those beatings your father gave you. He thought it would make a man of you. It was a waste of time." Her contempt knows no bounds. "You will never amount to much. Running little errands, trying to please me with your pathetic pandering. Well, I am not pleased. While you have been enjoying yourself with that woman, I have been in this cold room, hungry and alone." She extends her arm "Look at my hand. Its as cold as death."

Helmut looks up a little.

"Do you want to see me dead? Well? Answer me!"

"No."

Gisela is pleased. "Of course you don't. So why were you away so long?"

"You know I have no sense of time, mama."

"You have a watch. Dinner time was two hours ago."

"I'll get you a takeaway."

"I don't want a takeaway. I want a nice meal in a restaurant."

"It's late. It will have to be Indian or Chinese."

"See, that is how much you care for me. You are hopeless."

Helmut shakes his head. He just cannot win. "I'll get some wine too."

He picks up his coat, slips out the door.

Helmut returns to the boarding house, a take-away bag and two bottles of wine in his arms. There is the sound of music coming from Loretta's. He skips up the stairs and enters his room. Gisela is slumped on her bed asleep. Helmut picks up a small jar of sleeping pills at the side of the bed and shakes it to see how many pills are left. He smiles. He puts down the take-away, and leaves with the two wine bottles in his hands.

Helmut knocks on Loretta's door. She opens it. She is dressed in a beautiful Latin ballroom gown. "Bob. You're timing is perfect. I need a partner for this one."
She leads him inside. The music track that is playing is just coming to an end. She takes the wine out of his hands and places the bottles on a side table. She takes him by the hands, leads him a few feet, then takes up a tango stance with him.
"I hope you can tango, Bob?"
The music starts.
Helmut is not quite sure about the steps, but he follows Loretta. They tango. The space is limited, but they make a good attempt at following the music. To Loretta's surprise, Helmut is actually a very good dancer.
They enjoy their shared experience. It is bizarre, but also tender. Real delight shows on his face. He is truly happy for the briefest of moments. The track ends.
"You're a smashing dancer, Bob."
She reaches for the wine, snatches a bottle. Helmut takes her in his

arms, carries her to the bed.

"You're a crazy woman."

"I can tell you like crazy women."

He plunges his head under her dress. Loretta unscrews the bottle cap, takes a hit on the wine as Bob works his way up her inner thighs. "I knew you'd be back for more of me." She takes another slug.

"Get on to the bed, Bob. I'll do you at the same time?" She hands him the wine bottle to hold as she loosens his belt. She pushes his trousers off his buttocks and lunges on his erection.

There is a vibration from his shirt pocket. With his spare hand he reaches in and brings out Karin's cell phone. He pauses, looks down at Loretta eating on him. He slides his thumb across the screen and answers the call. A thin voice speaks.

"Karin. It's Maisie. Its on the news that Jacamo is dead." The phone is snatched out of his hand.

"I'm giving you head. The least you can do is pay attention." Loretta throws the phone on to the bed, throws her arms around his neck, and pushes her tongue into his mouth. He chokes, tries to throw her off, but her passion is too great to dislodge with ease. He raises his hand, takes her by the top of her head, and violently jerks her head backwards.

There is a snapping SOUND.

Loretta goes limp in his hands. His face turns to one of horror as he realises he has broken her neck. She drops away, falls heavily onto the bed beside the phone. He stands with the bottle of wine in his hand and this trousers around his ankles. In the background is the thin voice "Karin? Karin? Where are you?"

Helmut takes a long drink from the bottle, reaches forward and picks up the phone.

"Hello. Is that Maisie?"

"Yes. Who is this?"

"Its Father Bob,"

"Who?"

Helmut is now on speaker phone. As he talks he re-hitches his trousers – lays Loretta out on the bed, covers her as if she is asleep.

"I was just with Karin. She is very upset about Father Jacamo."

"Is she alright?"

"I think she may be suicidal."

"Can I speak with her?"

"She went for a walk."

"On her own? Why would you let her do that is she is suicidal? Why didn't she take her phone?"

"She was upset. She left her house keys too." Helmut pulls the keys from his trouser pocket.

"That's not good."

"Are you at the flat now?"

"Yes. What did you say your name was?"

"Father Bob. I'll drop the phone and keys off to you."

"Do you know the address?"

Helmut is looking at the crumpled utility bill. "We have it from the chapel records. I'll be there in half and hour.

He cuts the call.

Helmut quietly exits Loretta's - turns for the stairs. Gisela is standing there. "Mama. You scared me!"

"Where is she?"

"Who, mama?"

"Don't you come all innocent with me. I can smell sex. This whole house is pervaded with it." Gisela descends the stairs.

"No, mama. Don't go in there. She's

asleep."

"My ass!" Gisela pushes Helmut aside and enters Loretta's and strides into the bedroom. She reaches for the bedclothes. "Get up, you tart. You will leave my son alone!" She pulls the quilt off the bed. Loretta is lifeless with her eyes open.

Gisela pulls back in shock.

Helmut enters the room, closes the door behind him. "I'm sorry, mama. It was an accident."

Gisela slaps Helmut across the face. Hits him again, and again. Helmut grabs Gisela by her wrists, subdues her. "I will put her in the car ... take her somewhere!"

"Where???? Why are you like this!"

"Go upstairs, mama. We will leave in the morning."

"Leave for where? Its Germany all over again!"

"No its not, mama. Trust me. Please. Go back upstairs and pack."

*

Helmut places Loretta, wrapped in the bedspread, in the front boot of his Beetle. Gisela watches from the bay window. Helmut drives off.

Helmut is following the directions of his sat nav. He is completely focused on his driving. There is no remorse or doubt that he has done anything wrong. He is playing out the course of events that is weekend killing spree has taken him on.

As he pulls up outside a terrace row of rented flats inhabited by immigrants and students, he checks the house number with the utility bill – 117 Redhill Road. He switches off.

The opens the front bonnet and lifts Loretta out and throws her over his shoulder. He lumbers to number 117 and puts the key in the lock.

He enters the flat. It is a run down student place. There is heavy beat MUSIC playing.

The lounge is empty. Helmut sits Loretta on the sofa. He leaves the room.

In the kitchen Maisie and her girlfriend Patty are making out. They are doing some heavy petting, there hands are in all sorts of places. Helmut stands in the doorway watching.

Maisie looks up, gets immediately angry.

"Who the fuck are you?"

"Bob. From your voice, I take it you are Maisie?"

"Did you let yourself in?"

"Yep, sure did."

"He's no frickin' priest," Patty mutters.

"Shut up, Patty."

"Karin's phone and keys ..."

He lays them down on a counter top. "Karin's in the lounge."

Maisie's face brightens. Patty scowls. "I thought the bitch was going to kill herself?"

"Jealous are we?" Helmut asks.

"Frickin' right. She goes both ways that one. Flaunting her cunt at me every time she gets out the shower."

Maisie picks up Karin's cellphone, puts it in her blouse pocket, brushes past Helmut. He throws his arm around her neck, pulls her to him. "You go both ways too, darling?"

"Yeah, just like you priests."

"Your bitch got it right. I'm no priest."

"What are you, then? A social worker?"

"In my own way." Helmut thrusts a kitchen knife into Maisie's belly, leaves it there. Maisie falls to the floor as he takes hold of Patty - bends her over a counter.

"You ready to go both ways, sweetheart."

"You fucking animal!"

Helmut has his hand down the back of Patty's pants. "Jesus. What the fuck are you? Are you a boy? Are you a fucking boy?" He pulls out a strap-on dildo, throws it against the wall. He picks up the electric kettle, smashes Patty in the face. Patty reels against the sink. Helmut takes hold of her, pushes her head in a half- full sink of dish water – holds her there – drowns her.

Helmut turns. Maisie is gone.

Maisie has dragged herself into the lounge and is resting on the floor close to the sofa. She tugs on the bedspread.

"Karin ...."

Loretta rolls out of the bedspread, falls off the sofa and lands like a rag doll beside her. Maisie can't believe her eyes.

"Who the fuck are you!" She pushes Loretta away but soon realises Loretta is dead. She props herself up against the sofa, the knife still stuck in her belly. Helmut enters.

"There you are, swetheart."

"You are a sick bastard, you need to be locked up."

"I've been locked up before ... now I'm enjoying myself."

"Enjoying yourself? Why don't you just play video games like everybody else?"

"I'm not like everybody else. Here, let me help you with that."

Helmut pulls the knife out of Maisie's belly. She groans. Fresh blood starts to flow.

"I don't think the wound is fatal. You just won't be able to shit without using a bag."

"Just get it over with."

"You don't want to live to tell the tale?

"Do I look that stupid to believe that? Give me the fucking knife, I'll do it myself."

"Fighting talk. I like it. Maybe I should have met you before I met her." he points to Loretta. "We only ever did missionary."

"You're a scumbag. I'd never have gone out with you in a year of Sundays."

"Sure you would. I'm pretty hard to get rid of."

"Just give me the fucking knife, you bastard! I'm bleeding to death." She is immobilised, drained of all energy.

"It's painful to watch." He smiles sympathetically. "Look, I reckon you've got another twenty minutes. You might as well use it. You want a last cigarette?" Helmut puts a ciggy in Maisie's mouth, lights it.

"I always say that you should treat every moment as your last." He reaches into Maisie's pocket, pulls out Karin's phone, sets it on the far arm of the sofa. "Might as well leave you with some hope." He kisses her on the forehead.

"Bye, now." He leaves Maisie to her cigarette and slow death.

*

Gisela is sitting smoking in the passenger seat of the car. Helmut is tying the last of their belongings on to the roof-rack with bungee ropes. Helmut gets into the car. He smiles at his mother.

"Don't! I am never going to speak to you again."

"Oh mama. Its a long way to Blackpool." Gisela turns from him to look out of the window. Helmut laughs at his mother's behaviour. "Like you said, mama, I had a bad childhood."

He starts the car, puts it in gear. The car leaves the buzz of Brighton behind, moves into the growing fast flowing traffic, and disappears into the ribbons of cars and trucks on the motorway going north.

ROBBIE MOFFAT

The author was born and schooled in Glasgow. He took a degree in English language and Literature at Newcastle University. He began writing when he was seventeen and has had a career as a poet, novelist, playwright and screenwriter. He is best known for his feature film work in which he is also a director and producer.

His prose writing as been overshadowed by this. He wrote his first novel when he was twenty two and continued to write novels for the next twenty years. None of them were published.

The rediscovery of his prose work has lead to a recent spate of publications that has lead to a resurgence of interest in his prose writing.